Emma's Dancing Day

Story by Kimberly S. Hoffman

Illustrations by Em Vickers

PathBinder Publishing

COLUMBUS, INDIANA

Published by PathBinder Publishing
P.O. Box 2611
Columbus, IN 47202
www.PathBinderPublishing.com

Copyright © 2022 by Kimberly S. Hoffman
All rights reserved

Story by Kimberly S. Hoffman
Illustrations by Em Vickers

First published in 2016
Manufactured in the United States

ISBN: 978-1-955088-33-6
Library of Congress Control Number: 2022933849

All rights reserved. No part of this book may be reproduced or transmitted in any form whatsoever without prior written permission from the publisher except in the case of brief quotations embodied in critical articles and reviews.

This is a work of fiction. Unless otherwise indicated, all the names, characters, businesses, places, events and incidents in this book are either the product of the author's imagination or used in a fictitious manner. Any resemblance to actual persons, living or dead, or actual events is purely coincidental.

This Book Belongs to:

_____

To my "spider sisters" — Sarah & Rachel —
Books inspire and encourage us, cause us to ponder, keep us on the edge of our seats, and lead us on imaginary journeys to far-away lands.

May this book encourage us to never give up on the desires of our hearts.

Acknowledgements:

I thank God for giving me such a wonderful imagination. The story of Emma came from a little spider who visited me quite unexpectedly during ballet class.

Thank you to my husband, Paul, who assisted me with suggestions and edits through several drafts. It helps to have a published author in the house! He invited me to tag along to several author fairs, speaking engagements, and conventions. As I listened to him and other authors, I learned more of the art of writing and the desire to publish my story grew. Thank you for teaching me, loving me, and encouraging me throughout the process. I cannot thank you enough for your faith in me and my abilities.

Thank you to my oldest daughter, Sarah, for her comments and edits of an early draft. I appreciate your straightforwardness. You were a huge asset in honing my story.

Thank you to my daughters, Rachel and Sarah, for our times of make believe and for the story times we enjoyed. You have awesome imaginations and story-telling abilities. I treasure those times in my heart. I love you both. You make me one proud mama!

I want to acknowledge my friends, Debbie and Joe, for their encouragement during this process. It helps to have cheerleaders! Thank you both! You will never know how your kind words strengthened me.

Thank you to my publisher, Debi, for believing in my story and taking a chance on an unpublished author.

And though my mom has passed, I am thankful for the countless trips to the library to bring home armloads of books. Thank you, Mom; you fueled my love for reading and writing. You always let me know what a gift reading was.

Across the floor of the Bluebell Ballet,

Sunbeams shone at end of day.

A tiny spider spun and twirled,

As she watched the ballerina girls.

EMMA'S DANCING DAY

"I wish I could dance lovely and fine.

To whirl and leap would be divine.

"But look at me! It is hard to dance.

With so many legs, do I have a chance?"

EMMA'S DANCING DAY

A graceful, young girl spun in place,

A look of delight upon her face.

Emma could not wait to try,

To dance with joy made her sigh.

EMMA'S DANCING DAY

So she raised up on her forty toes;

Spun so quickly, she fell on her nose.

EMMA'S DANCING DAY

Tears filled her eyes

and ran down her cheeks.

Her knees stung sharply

and her legs felt weak.

EMMA'S DANCING DAY

Slowly, so slowly she crossed the floor.

Arrived at home, and closed the door.

EMMA'S DANCING DAY

"Well, there you are!" her mother said.

"It's time to eat, then bath and bed."

EMMA'S DANCING DAY

Emma sat down to eat fried fly,

Laid down her fork and began to cry!

"Mommy! Daddy! Tell me why!"

EMMA'S DANCING DAY

"I wish I could twirl and glide all day,

But how can I, with eight legs in the way?"

"I watch the ballerinas while they learn.

But, tell me when will it be my turn?"

EMMA'S DANCING DAY

Daddy took his girl upon three knees,

Kissed her head, "Emma, listen to me."

"God made you just the way you are.

Eight legs are special. They'll take you far."

EMMA'S DANCING DAY

"If in your heart you want to dance,

Go to class and take a chance."

"God plants a seed within our hearts.

It grows quite big if we just start."

"Your gift brings joy to everyone;

And gives you peace when day is done."

EMMA'S DANCING DAY

Mama hugged her girl so tight.

"Emma, dear, it will be all right."

EMMA'S DANCING DAY

Emma said her prayers and went to bed,

With dreams of pink tutus in her head.

EMMA'S DANCING DAY

When morning's sunbeams touched her face,

She popped out of bed and to breakfast she raced.

EMMA'S DANCING DAY

"Mama, hurry,

I've got to eat.

Put on my tutu

and shoes on eight feet!"

EMMA'S DANCING DAY

Emma dressed in a flash

and hurried out the door.

Her heart nearly bursting

as she dashed 'cross the floor.

EMMA'S DANCING DAY

She quietly crept up beside one girl,

Took a deep breath,

EMMA'S DANCING DAY

KIMBERLY S. HOFFMAN

Ready,

Set,

Twirl!

EMMA'S DANCING DAY

ABOUT THE AUTHOR

Kimberly S. Hoffman not only writes stories with themes of overcoming obstacles, thinking outside the box regarding disabilities, self-sacrifice and more, but she speaks on these topics at schools, libraries and civic clubs, often incorporating dance into the programs.

Kimberly grew up in Columbus, Indiana, where trips to the library happened nearly every week of her childhood. She loves to read and thinks the library is a wonderful place to be. She knows that books can teach us, transport us to new realms, inspire us, cause us to cry, or make us fall over laughing.

Kimberly loves to dance and can often be found dancing around her house (and sometimes in public), creating choreography to whatever song is playing. She also creates essential oil diffuser jewelry, which she sells through Queen Bee Designs.

She is married to Paul J. Hoffman, an author and publisher. Together, they have six children and many grand-fur and feather babies.

Be sure to find Kimberly on Facebook - Kimberly S Hoffman-Author, Twitter - @SpiderAuthor, Instagram - @kimberlyhoffman_author or at her blog - kimberlyhoffmanblog.wordpress.com, and invite her to speak to your group. She can also be reached at khoffmanauthor@gmail.com.

Kimberly's other books:
Sigmund Stanley Spider Squared
Pete the Brave
Love, Hope: Children Express Their Emotions During the Coronavirus Pandemic
The Red Coat: Giving and Gratitude During The Great Depression
Cleo and Roger Discover Columbus, Indiana
Cleo and Roger Discover the Art of Columbus, Indiana

This title is available in paperback, hardback, and e-book.

Visit us at www.PathBinderPublishing.com

CPSIA information can be obtained
at www.ICGtesting.com
Printed in the USA
BVHW021404290322
632750BV00005B/449